Little Bear

Note

Once a reader can recognize and identify the 16 words used to tell this story, he or she will be able to read successfully the entire book. These 16 words are repeated throughout the story, so that young readers will be able to easily recognize the words and understand their meaning.

The 16 words used in this book are:

bear	I	please	what
cheese	little	potatoes	will
eat	not	some	would
honey	peas	tomatoes	you

ISBN 0-516-23802-7

Text copyright © 1990 by Nancy Hall, Inc. Illustrations copyright © 1990 by Lisa McCue. All rights reserved. Published by Scholastic Inc., 555 Broadway, New York, NY 10012, by arrangement with Orchard Books, Inc. SCHOLASTIC and associated logos are trademarks and/or registered trademarks of Scholastic Inc.

12 11 10 9 8 7 6 5   4 5 6/0

Printed in the U.S.A.

First Scholastic printing, March 2001

Little Bear

Written by Diane Namm
Illustrated by Lisa McCue

SCHOLASTIC INC.
New York Toronto London Auckland Sydney
Mexico City New Delhi Hong Kong

Little Bear, Little Bear, would you eat potatoes?

Little Bear, Little Bear,

would you eat some peas?

Little Bear, Little Bear,
would you eat tomatoes?

Little Bear, Little Bear,

would you eat some cheese?

I will not eat potatoes!

I will not eat some peas!

I will not eat tomatoes!

I will not eat some cheese!

Not potatoes?
Not some peas?

Not tomatoes?
Not some cheese?

What will you eat, Little Bear?

I will eat some honey ...

please!